Hello, Sweetie Pie

Carl Norac   Illustrated by Claude K. Dubois

SCHOLASTIC INC.

New York   Toronto   London   Auckland   Sydney
Mexico City   New Delhi   Hong Kong   Buenos Aires

Whenever Lola is happy, she sings.
It's her special way of being cheerful.
Lola felt like singing today.
Her first day of class had been lots of fun.

After school, Lola saw her friend Lulu.
"Lola," her friend asked, "what do your parents call you?"

"It depends," answered Lola with glee.
"Sometimes they call me their babycake,
or their sweetie pie, or their fairy princess."

Lulu and the other children burst out laughing.

Lola didn't feel like singing anymore.
Why are they making fun of me? she wondered.
I bet everyone has a silly nickname. I'm going to check!

"Excuse me, sir," said Lola to a police officer.
"What did your parents call you when you were little?"

"My little chick," answered the policeman. "Why do you ask?"
"Oh, no reason," said Lola.

Lola asked the baker the same question.
"My little bread ball," said the baker with a bashful smile.

Lola passed a woman whose baby was crying and kicking.
"Hush, hush, my angel," said the mother soothingly.
Strange angel! thought Lola.

Lola began to sing again. She was feeling much better. Everyone *did* have a nickname!

At the bus stop, Lola heard laughter behind her.
"There's the fairy princess! Kootchy-koo, little babycake!"
the children teased.

Lola didn't want to face Lulu and the other kids.
Instead, she walked all the way home—
without whistling, without singing.

"Hello, babycake," said Daddy as he opened the door for her.
"I'm not a baby anymore. I'm a giant!" cried Lola.

"Hello, my little fairy princess," said Mommy.
"I'm not a fairy. I'm a witch!" shouted Lola.

Mommy and Daddy were worried.
"What's wrong, precious sweetie pie?" they asked.

"I *am* your sweetie pie!" Lola exclaimed, jumping into their arms. That was one nickname she couldn't resist.

The next day, as Lola headed back to school,
she wasn't thinking about Lulu and all her teasing anymore.

In the school yard, Lulu found her right away.
"I'm sorry about yesterday," Lulu said. "I was jealous
because at my house, nobody uses little nicknames."
"Oh, how sad!" cried Lola.

"Don't worry," Lulu said, smiling.
"Last night I talked to my parents about it
and we worked it all out."
"Great!" said Lola. "So what are they calling you?"

"It depends," said Lulu proudly.
"Babycake, sweetie pie, or fairy princess."
"That can't be," cried Lola.
"Those names are mine—only mine!"

In class, Lola pouted.
I'm the precious sweetie pie, she thought, *not Lulu.*

Then Lola got tired of pouting. She thought hard.
Silly little nicknames were for everyone, after all!

"Lulu, you know what?" Lola said.
"I'd like to teach you how to sing."

Now whenever Lola and Lulu are happy, they sing.
It's their special way of being cheerful.

For Léa   For Aymeric
—C.N.   —C.D.K.

ISBN 0-439-25191-5

Copyright © 1999 by *l'école des loisirs*, Paris.
English translation copyright © 2000 by Random House, Inc.
All rights reserved. Published by Scholastic Inc., 555 Broadway, New York, NY 10012,
by arrangement with Random House Children's Books, a division of Random House, Inc.
SCHOLASTIC and associated logos are trademarks and/or
registered trademarks of Scholastic Inc.

12 11 10 9 8 7 6 5 4 3 2 1   1 2 3 4 5 6/0

Printed in Mexico   49

First Scholastic printing, October 2001

The text of this book is set in 16-point Gill Sans.